Postman Pat® and the Giant Snowball

D1079474

SIMON AND SCHUSTER

It was a snowy day in Greendale. Pat was making his way slowly over the slippery roads to Ted Glen's watermill. He had a special delivery for him.

Pat got the funny-shaped parcel from the van, and knocked on Ted's door.

"Oh dear, no answer," he sighed. "Ted has to sign for this. I'll have to find him."

On his way back along the country lane, Pat saw the children whizzing down the hill on their snowboards.

"Look at me, Dad!" called Julian, zooming after Meera.

"You're all ever so good," admired Pat. "I'd like a go at that myself! But right now I have to find Ted Glen. Have any of you seen him, by any chance?"

Nobody had seen Ted.

"Doesn't he help Ajay on the train today, Dad?" suggested Julian.

"Good thinking, Julian. I'll go and see."

When Pat arrived at the station, Ajay was firing up the steam train.

"Takes more than a bit of snow to stop the Greendale Rocket getting through!" he remarked proudly.

"Any sign of Ted?" asked Pat, handing Ajay his post.

"Not yet, Pat."

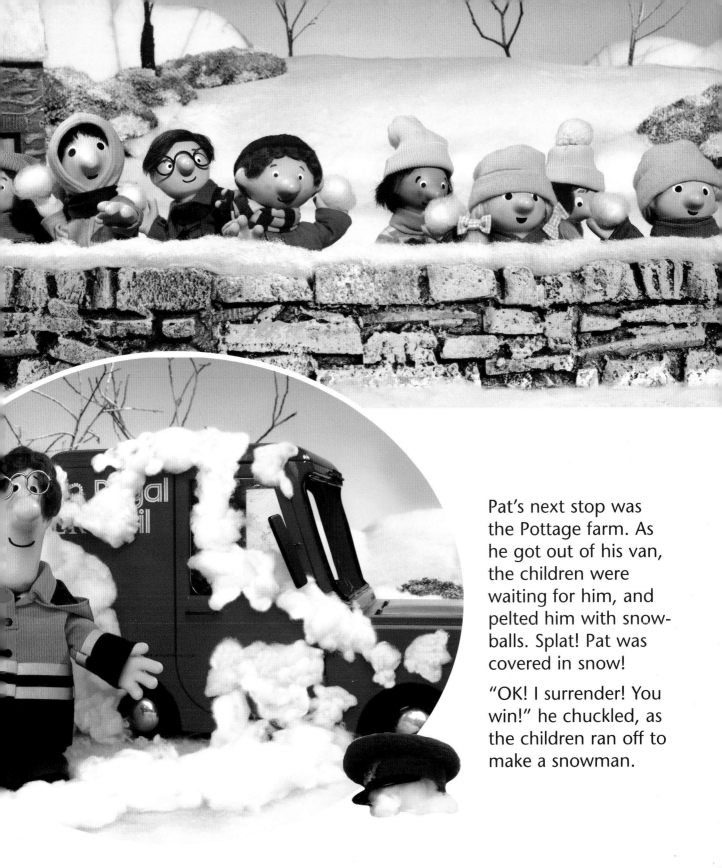

Pat's next stop was the Pottage farm. As he got out of his van, the children were waiting for him, and pelted him with snowballs. Splat! Pat was covered in snow!

"OK! I surrender! You win!" he chuckled, as the children ran off to make a snowman.

The snowball got bigger and bigger as the children pushed it up the hill.
"Heave! Heave!" Bill and Sarah kept on pushing until . . .

"Stop!" Charlie cried out. "If the snowball rolls down the other side of the hill, it'll land on the railway!"

Too late! Out of control, the giant snowball rolled faster and faster, crashed through the fence and landed right on the track.

"Oh no!" cried Julian. "The train is due any minute. That snowball's big enough to make it come off the rails!"

"Quick! We need to get help!" said Bill. "My house is closest. Julian, Meera and Sarah, you come with me. Kate, Tom, Charlie and Lucy, you run along the bank and watch out for the train."

Meanwhile, at the station, the train was ready to leave!

"All aboard!" called Ajay.

Pat was delivering the post at Bill's house when the children arrived, out of breath.

"Dad!" yelled Julian. "We made a giant snowball for our snowman . . ."

"And it rolled right down the hill," squealed Meera.

"Onto the railway track," gasped Sarah.

"We've got to stop the train!" wailed Bill.

"Oh dear! said Pat. "My van's hopeless in all this snow. We'll never make it in time. Unless . . ."

Pat had a brainwave. He leapt onto a snowboard, and whizzed off, using Ted's parcel to balance. "Follow me!" he called to the children.

Pat skidded, swerved and somersaulted downhill. The children were impressed!

Meanwhile, the train was getting closer.

"Toot-toot!"

Charlie, Tom, Lucy and Katie waved and yelled as they saw it come round the corner. "Stop, Ajay, stop!"

But Ajay couldn't hear them – he just waved back!

Pat arrived in the nick of time. Attaching his jacket to Ted's parcel, he waved it frantically to and fro.

"Something's wrong, Ted!" Ajay pulled on the brakes. The wheels locked and the train screeched to a halt.

The bumpers knocked gently into the giant snowball, leaving a large mound of snow.

"Oh my!" gasped Reverend Timms.

"That was close!" gulped Ajay.

The children clapped and cheered.

"We did it, we did it!"

"We certainly did!" grinned Pat. "Thanks to Ted's parcel!"

"There you are, Ted!" said Pat. "Sign here, please!"

"Aha, my new shovel!" smiled Ted.

"Just what we need to clear all this snow away!" chuckled Ajay.

They shovelled the snow in no time.

"Well done, every-body," Ajay grinned. "All aboard!"

"Well, I'd best check Jess is all right," said Pat. "Mind you stay away from the railway track in future," he warned the children.

"Yes, Dad," said Julian . . . and – THUMP! – threw a snowball at Pat's back!

"Want to play, do you?" laughed Pat. "Take that then!"

And they all had the best snowball fight ever!

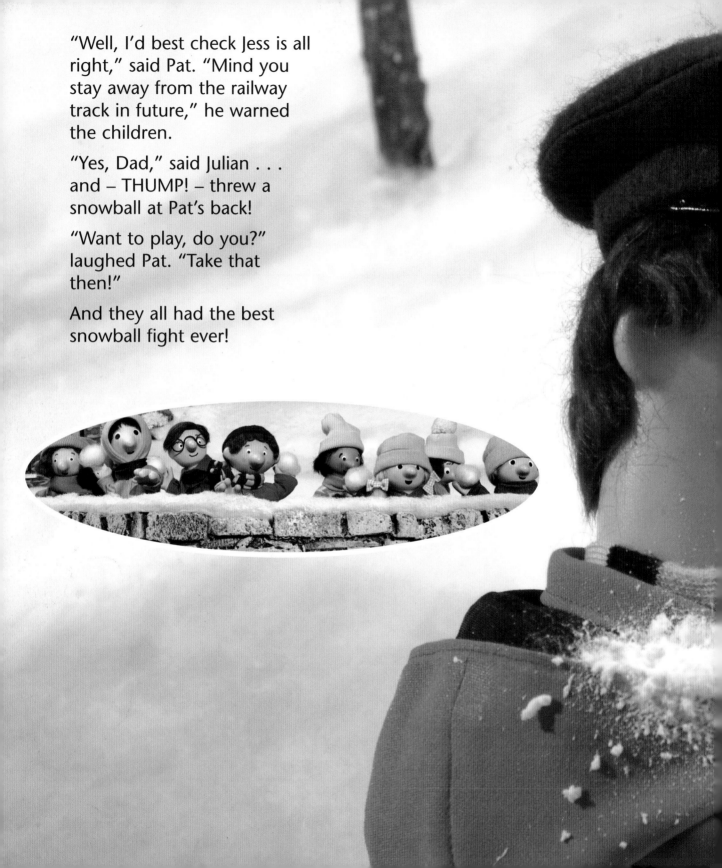

SIMON AND SCHUSTER
First published in 2006 in Great Britain by Simon & Schuster UK Ltd
Africa House, 64-78 Kingsway
London WC2B 6AH

Postman Pat® © 2006 Woodland Animations, a division of Entertainment Rights PLC
Licensed by Entertainment Rights PLC
Original writer John Cunliffe
From the original television design by Ivor Wood
Royal Mail and Post Office imagery is used by kind permission of Royal Mail Group plc
All rights reserved

Text by Alison Ritchie © 2006 Simon & Schuster UK Ltd

A CIP catalogue record for this book is available from the British Library upon request

ISBN 141691126X
EAN 9781416911265

Printed in China

1 3 5 7 9 10 8 6 4 2